words
stories

Chicken Licken

Stories adapted by Shirley Jackson
Illustrated by Angela Terris
Series designed by Jeannette Slater

Copyright © 1999 Egmont World Limited.
All rights reserved.
Published in Great Britain by Egmont World Limited,
Deanway Technology Centre, Wilmslow Road,
Handforth, Cheshire SK9 3FB
Printed in Germany
ISBN 0 7498 4360 8

Chicken Licken

nut

sky

king

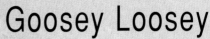
Goosey Loosey

Henny
Penny

Turkey
Lurkey

Foxy
Loxy

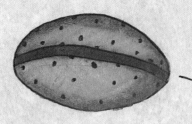

Once upon a time,
a nut fell.

It fell on Chicken
Licken.

new words

"The sky is falling in,"
said Chicken Licken.
"I am going to tell
the king."

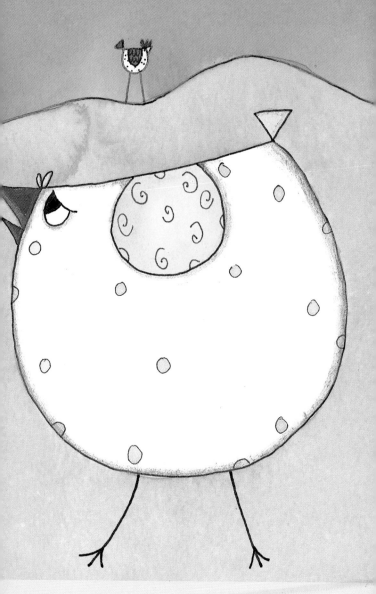

w words **is falling am going tell**

Chicken Licken met
Henny Penny.

"The sky is falling in,"
said Chicken Licken.
"I am going to tell
the king."

ew word **met**

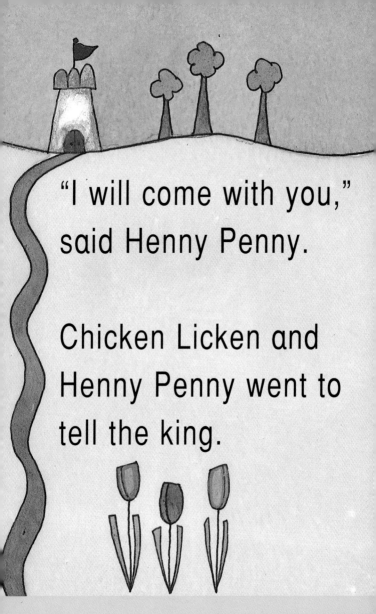

"I will come with you,"
said Henny Penny.

Chicken Licken and
Henny Penny went to
tell the king.

But then Chicken Licken and Henny Penny met Goosey Loosey.

"The sky is falling in," said Chicken Licken and Henny Penny. "We are going to tell the king."

ew words   **But   then   We   are**

"I will come with you," said Goosey Loosey.

Chicken Licken, Henny Penny and Goosey Loosey went to tell the king.

new words

But then Chicken
Licken, Henny Penny
and Goosey Loosey
met Turkey Lurkey.

"The sky is falling in," they said. "We are going to tell the king."

ew word **they**

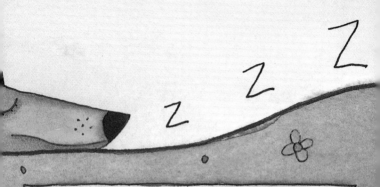

"I will come with you,"
said Turkey Lurkey.

Chicken Licken, Henny
Penny, Goosey Loosey
and Turkey Lurkey
went to tell the king.

o new words

But then Chicken
Licken, Henny Penny,
Goosey Loosey and
Turkey Lurkey met
Foxy Loxy.

"The sky is falling
in," they said.
"We are going
to tell the king."

"Come with me," said Foxy Loxy.

And that was the end of Chicken Licken, Henny Penny, Goosey Loosey and Turkey Lurkey!